The Hibernating House

By Sandy Leahy & Kathy Tarentino

Sh, Sh, Sh!

Quiet as a mouse

This is the hibernating house . . .

Illustrated by Kristine Daniels

First published by Dog Ear Publishing
4010 W. 86th Street, Ste H
Indianapolis, IN 46268
www.dogearpublishing.net

ISBN: 978-1-4575-1753-2

This book is printed on acid-free paper.

This book is a work of fiction.

Printed in the United States of America

Dedicated to our grandchildren

Hannah • Ava

Shawn • Kyle

Giuliana • Gabriella

Thanks to the Easy Breezy,

where the Leahy family and friends have vacationed for more than twenty years.
Located on the island of Martha's Vineyard, nestled in nature,
this quaint Massachusetts cottage keeps a watchful eye
on the seaside community as it changes from season to season.

As Sandy and Kathy sat rocking on the porch,
reminiscing about summer fun with their families and friends,
regretting that it was time to leave,
the inspiration for **The Hibernating House** took hold.

Seasons may change in this summer town,
but the memories will last a lifetime.

Sh, Sh, Sh!

Quiet as a mouse

This is the hibernating house . . .

It's fall in this little summer town,

Time to put the shutters down,

Board up the windows, lock up the doors,

Say goodbye to another season

     of sand on the floors.

It's time for this little old house to sleep,

Get ready for the winter deep,

Farewell to this house we hold so dear,

Won't see you again until next year.

You'll be lonely while we're away,

No little children at work or at play,

We'll be back for the season that's best,

Now it's time for you to rest.

Sleepy house now close your eyes,

"Winter is coming!" the cold air cries,

Days get short, nights grow long,

This house is ready for the winter's song.

And the house is sleeping.

Sh, sh, sh!

Quiet as a mouse

This is the sleeping house . . .

Lonely house sits still upon the bluff,

Ferries come and go on the ocean rough,

Bringing cars and people, but only a few,

Winter is here, storms start to brew.

Skies are gray, cold winds blow,

The house can sense frigid waves below,

Frost on the roof, snow on the lawn,

Where have all the people gone?

"Closed for the season," the signs all say,

Downtown shops are empty, nothing on display,

No cars about, sidewalks bare,

Can you feel the cold in the air?

Flying horses standing still,

Sleeping through the winter's chill,

Only the sound of creaking floors,

They're waiting for spring, just open those doors!

And the house is waiting.

Look, look, look!

Mr. Sun is getting stronger.

The house is hibernating no longer . . . .

Suddenly one day, without any warning,

The house begins to wake, stretching and yawning,

Unlock the doors, open the shutters,

All at once, the hibernating house flutters.

Open your eyelashes, at first just a wink,

It's time to get ready for spring, don't you think?

Let in the fresh air, call the cleaning crew,

Mop the floors, dust the house through and through.

Shine the windows, refresh the curtains,

Now you'll wake up, of this I am certain,

Hear the vacuum's mighty roar,

Listen to the activity coming through the door.

The hum of motors passing the drive,

Wake up! It's spring! All is coming alive!

Flowers budding, lawns turning green,

Soon the family will be back on the scene.

And the house is waking!

"Smile, smile, smile,"

The house says with a grin.

"Hibernation is over, let the summer begin. . ."

Car doors slamming, luggage in the drive,

Hurray for summer, the family has arrived!

Familiar voices fill the air, little feet go pitter-patter,

The house is full of laughter,

    that's all that really matters.

Children calling out, "May we go to the beach?"

Can't wait one moment longer

    for surf and sand to reach,

Bringing pails and shovels, towels and coolers, too,

There is not one other thing

    that we would rather do.

Wet towels on the porch rail, all colors, deep and bright,

Makes the house feel lived in, see it smiling with delight,

Time for celebration, drape the house in red, white, and blue,

Cut the watermelon, light the barbeque.

Families gather on the porch, *oohs* and *aahs* we hear,

Feel the excitement from the crowd, the parade is getting near,

Saluting to the soldiers, waving flags up high,

The house is feeling patriotic, it's the 4th of July!

And the house is alive!

Scurry, scurry, scurry!

A new season is dawning.

The sleepy house is yawning . . .

One more month of summer, crowds still fill the town,

Days are getting shorter, starting the fall countdown,

Take one last hop on jetty rocks,

Time for sweatshirts, shoes, and socks.

Fill the red wagon up with treasures,

To remind us of our summer pleasures,

Say goodbye to special friends,

So much to do before vacation ends.

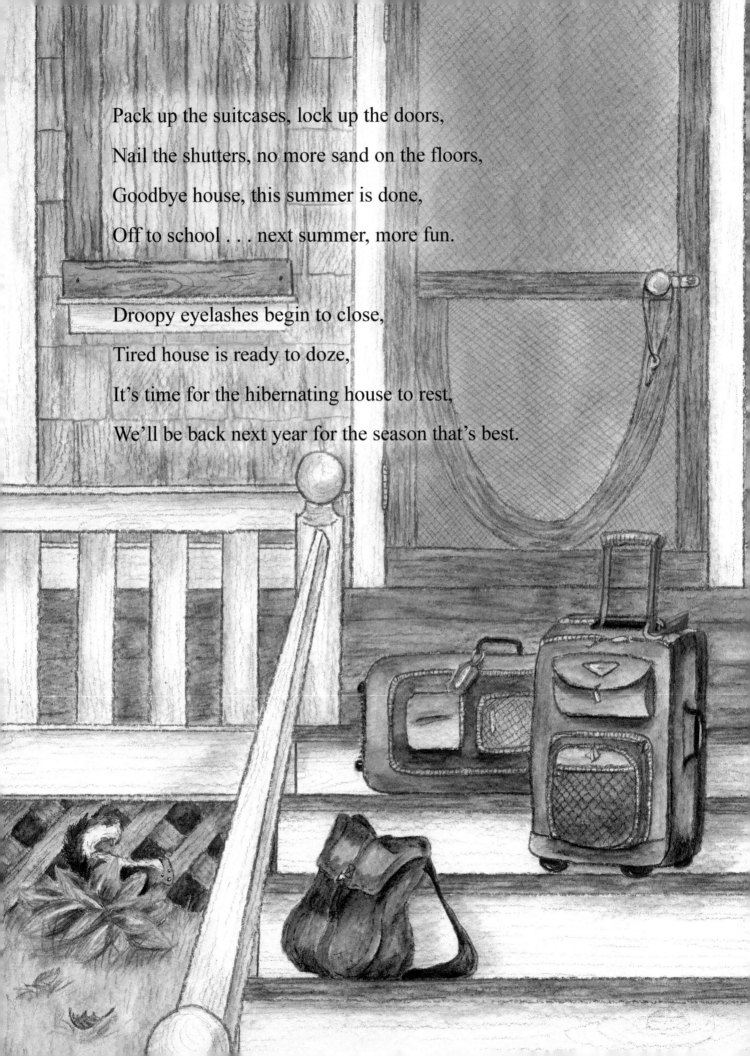

Pack up the suitcases, lock up the doors,

Nail the shutters, no more sand on the floors,

Goodbye house, this summer is done,

Off to school . . . next summer, more fun.

Droopy eyelashes begin to close,

Tired house is ready to doze,

It's time for the hibernating house to rest,

We'll be back next year for the season that's best.

Sh, sh, sh!

Quiet as a mouse

This is the hibernating house.

See you next year!

CPSIA information can be obtained
at www.ICGtesting.com
Printed in the USA
LVIC040146140313
323597LV00003BB